Dear Mum
This one is for you with all my love.
Slumber deep, my darling.
xxx D

Goodnight

Goodnight, Baby Bat! A DOUBLEDAY BOOK 978 0 385 60632 5 Published in Great Britain by Doubleday, an imprint of Random House Children's Books

This edition published 2007 1 3 5 7 9 10 8 6 4 2

Addresses for companies within The Random House Group Limited can be found at: www.randomhouse.co.uk/offices.htm THE RANDOM HOUSE GROUP Limited Reg. No. 954009

A CIP catalogue record for this book is available from the British Library. Printed in China

Baby Bat

Debi Gliori

DOUBLEDAY

Bedtime, Baby Bat.
Time to brush your teeth
and your face.
Have you washed behind
your wings?

Thought not.

Pardon me?

You won't slip into bed until your *snail* is tucked in?

Slither into your shell.

Night-night, Snail.

What a wiggly, giggly Baby Bat.

Why so squiggly?
You can't keep still until
Caterpillar's tucked in?

Squiggle and squirm,
let's tuck her in.
A hug for the bug.
No wiggling your toes,
Caterpillar.

You are wide awake, my Baby Bat.
Whatever is the matter?

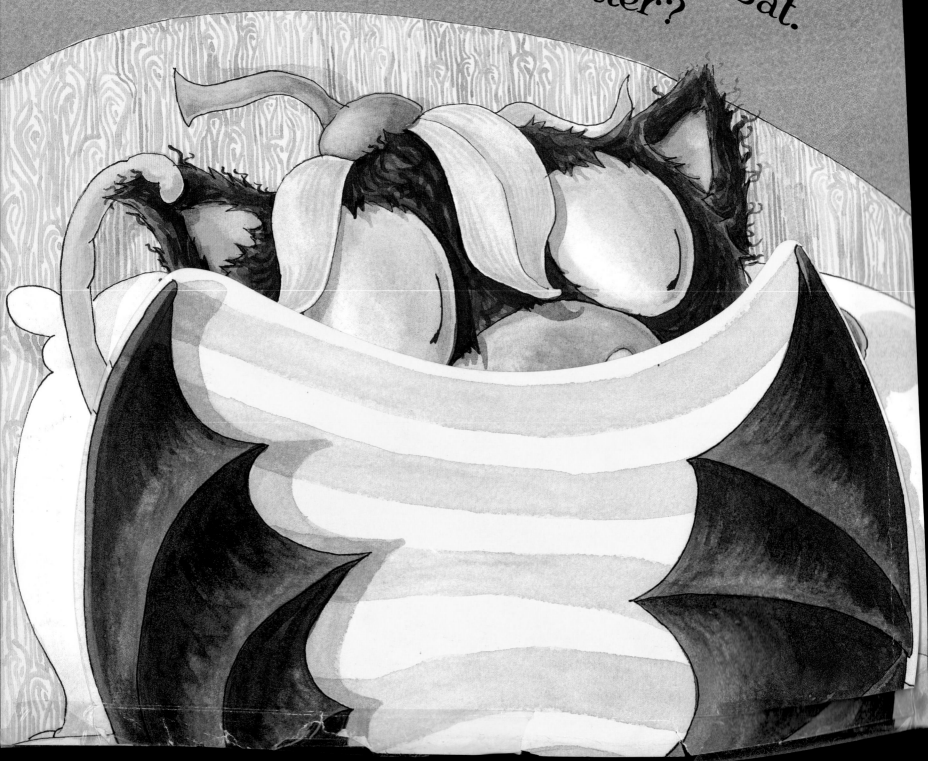

You can't close your eyes until Spider is tucked in?

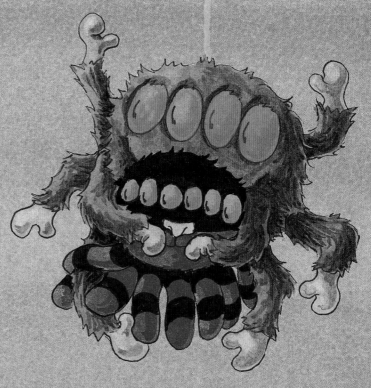

If you insist. Give Spider a kiss.
NOW. Close your eyes,
eyes,
eyes,
eyes,
eyes,
eyes.

It *is* bright, the moonlight.
No. You don't need moon glasses.
Oh, Baby Bat. Go to sleep.
We can't tuck up Moon.
She's too far away for a hug.
She's too cold for a kiss.
She's too big for a quilt.

But she's
just perfect
for a cloud.

Go to sleep,
my Baby Bat.
Snail is tucked up,
Caterpillar and
Spider too.
Even Moon is
tucked up in
her bed
of clouds.

The whole
world is
sleeping.

Look., Baby Bat.
Now even the world
is being tucked in.

Flake

by

flake

White

upon

white

Flake

by

flake

White

upon

white

Softly

softly

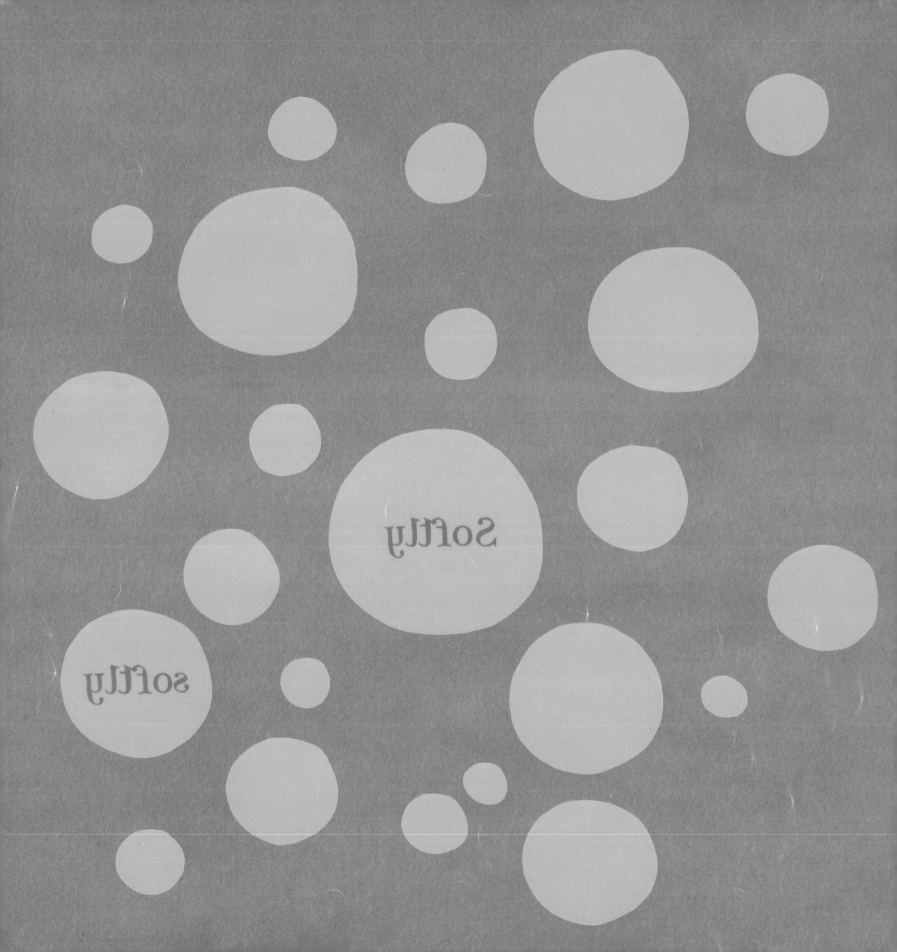

under a quilt of snow.

And now it's your turn.
Go to sleep, my Baby Bat.
Slumber deep,
my darling.